W9-AVC-418

A Piece Of Chalk

Jennifer A. Ericsson

Illustrations by Michelle Shapiro

A NEAL PORTER BOOK

ROARING BROOK PRESS

NEW MILFORD, CONNECTICUT

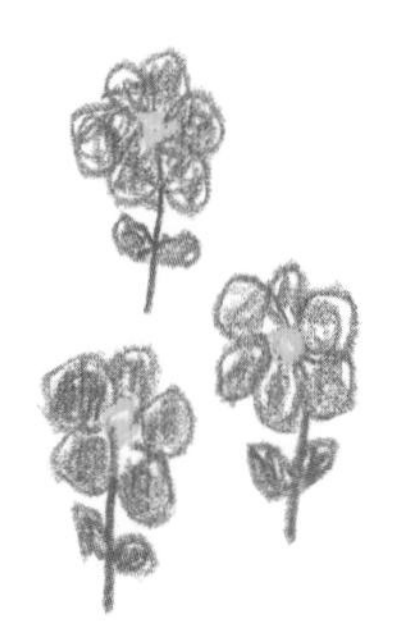

For Annie B. Ericsson & Beth L. Blair — my two favorite artists—J.A.E.

For my son, Nathan, who constantly inspires my creative curiosity—M.S.

A Neal Porter Book

Published by Roaring Brook Press

Roaring Brook Press is a division of Holtzbrinck Publishing Holdings Limited Partnership

143 West Street, New Milford, Connecticut 06776

www.roaringbrookpress.com

Distributed in Canada by H. B. Fenn and Company, Ltd.

Library of Congress Cataloging-in-Publication Data

Ericsson, Jennifer A.

A piece of chalk / by Jennifer A. Ericsson ; illustrated by Michelle Shapiro. — 1st ed.

p. cm.

"A Neal Porter book."

Summary: A little girl creates a colorful chalk drawing on her driveway.

ISBN-13: 978-1-59643-057-0 ISBN-10: 1-59643-057-5

[1. Drawing—Fiction. 2. Color—Fiction.] I. Shapiro, Michelle, 1961- ill. II. Title.

PZ7.E72584Pi 2007 [E]—dc22 2006032178

Roaring Brook Press books are available for special promotions and premiums.

For details, contact: Director of Special Markets, Holtzbrinck Publishers.

Printed in China

First edition September 2007

10 9 8 7 6 5 4 3 2 1

I have a box of chalk,
A brand new box,
With long perfect sticks
All smooth and dusty.

The driveway is my chalkboard,
A long, wide space

Just waiting—
Waiting for me.

I take a piece of chalk,
A brick red one.
Red is a wall
Stretching from side to side.

CHALK

I take a piece of chalk,
A lemon yellow one.
Yellow is the sun
Shining brightly up above.

I take a piece of chalk,
A spring green one.
Green is the grass
Sprouting near the wall.

I take a piece of chalk,
A dirt brown one.
Brown are the birds
Hopping through the grass.

I take a piece of chalk,
A fiery orange one.

Orange is the cat
Leaping at the birds.

I take a piece of chalk,
A snowy white one.
White is the dog
Jumping over the wall.

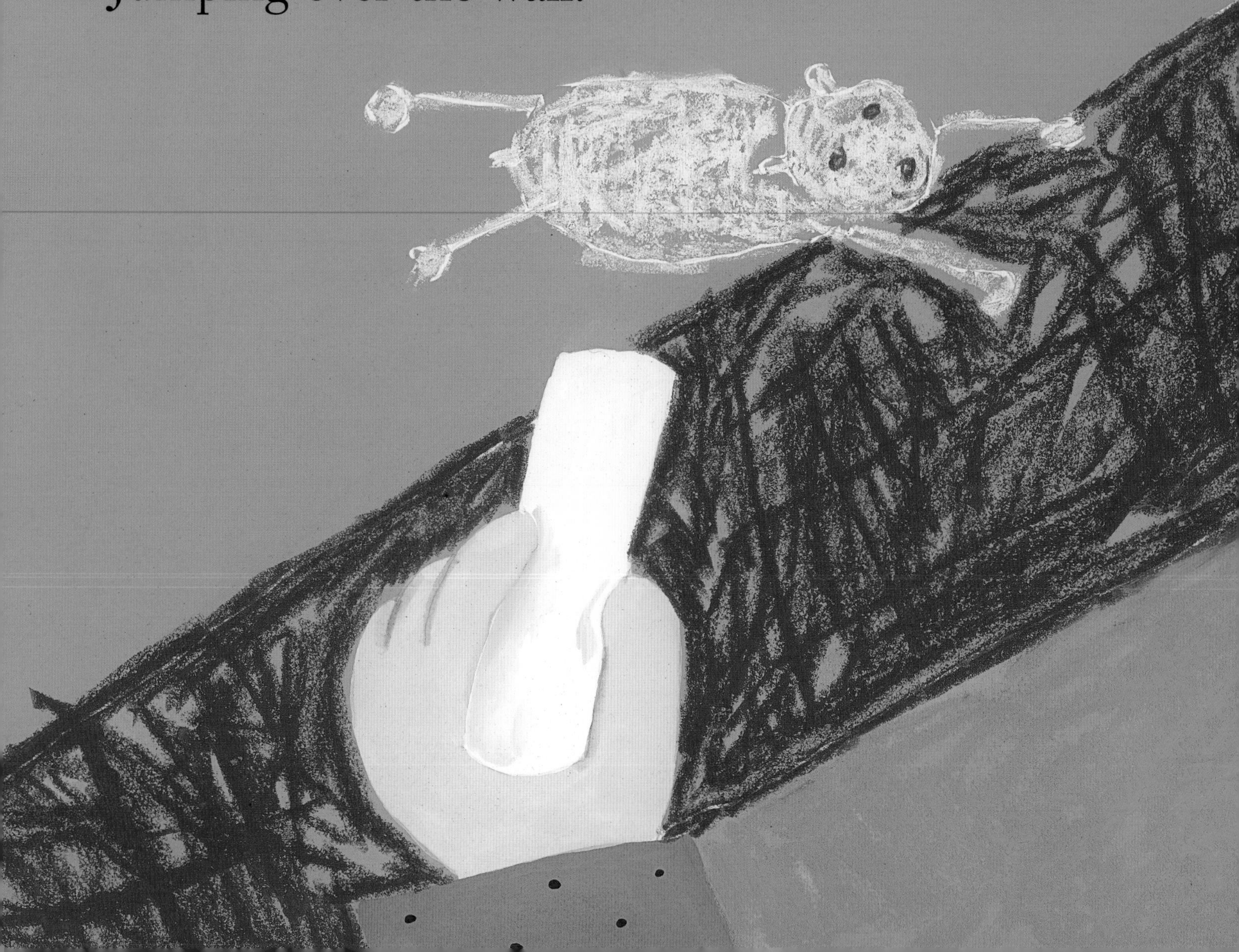

I take a piece of chalk,
A petal pink one.
Pink are the stripes
On a little girl's clothes.

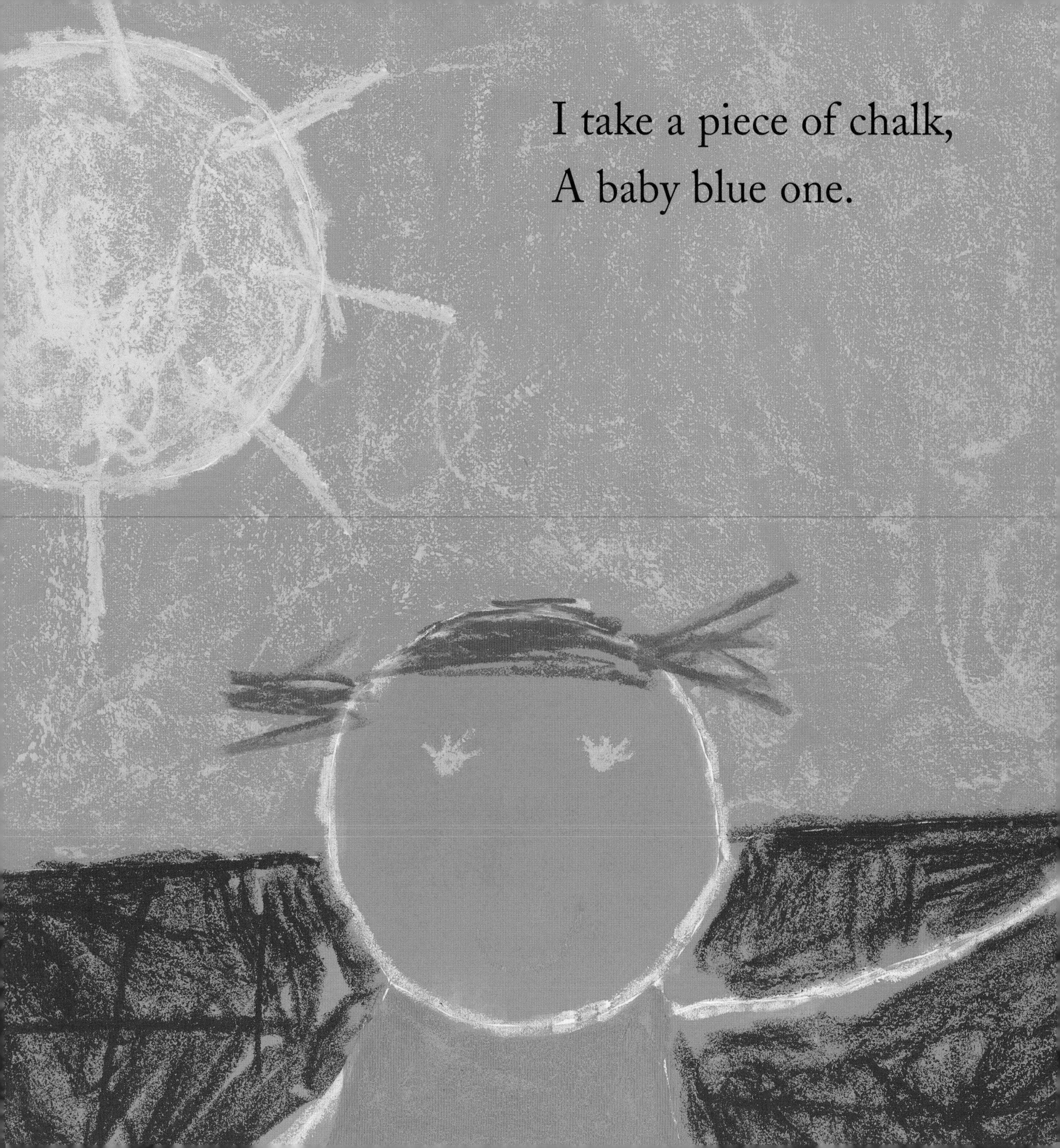

I take a piece of chalk,
A baby blue one.

Blue is the sky
And the little girl's eyes.

I take a piece of chalk,
A stormy gray one.
Gray are the clouds
And the rain that starts to fall.

It splatters the wall.
It scatters the birds.
It drips on the grass.

And it drops on me.

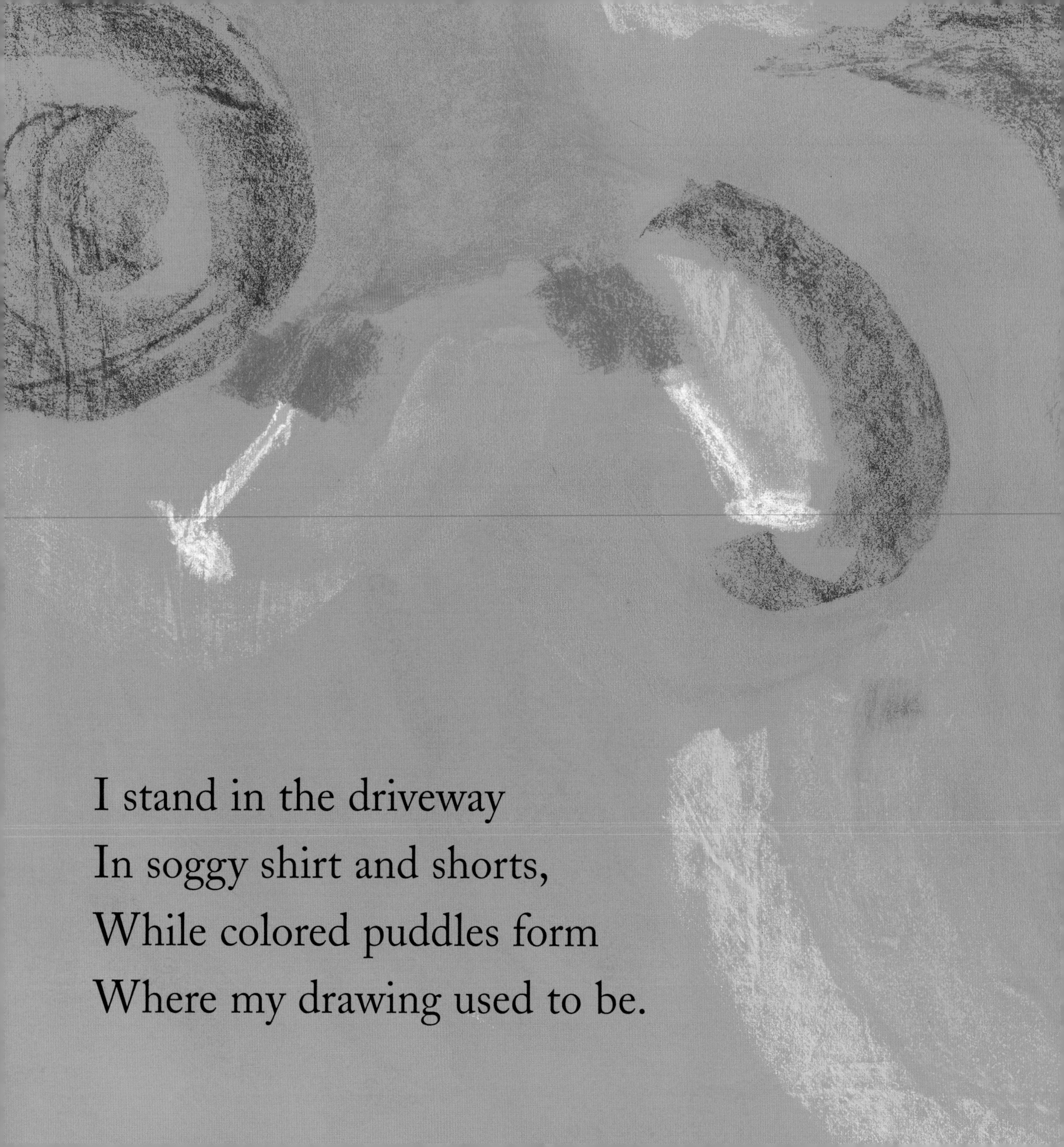

I stand in the driveway
In soggy shirt and shorts,
While colored puddles form
Where my drawing used to be.

I frown for a moment
As the colors run together,
But then the sun comes out
And I feel a smile grow.

For I have a box of chalk.
I can draw new pictures.
I also have two rainbows—
In the sky and at my feet.